Act Normal

And Don't Tell Anyone About

The Ladder Into Space

By Christian Darkin

First Printing 2016 by Rational Stories

www.RationalStories.com

The illustrations are by the author but use some elements for which thanks and credits go to www.obsidiandawn.com, kuschelirmel- stock, Theshelfs and waywardgal at Deviantart.com
Story and illustrations by © Christian Darkin.

CHAPTER 1

I don't like fairy tales, but especially, I don't like, "Jack And The Beanstalk".

I super especially don't like Jack.

All fairy tales have a moral, but the moral of, "Jack And The Beanstalk" seems to be that if you're really silly and you give your cow away for a couple of beans, it's OK as long as you steal from the giant and then kill him at the end.

I don't think being stupid, and stealing and killing is a very good moral for a story.

People in this story:

Me: I am Jenny. I do like making things, and I do like space, so this is my ideal sort of adventure. I don't like having tanks pointing their guns at me so much, but when you do the sort of things I do, that will happen sometimes.

Adam: Adam is my little brother. Adam likes tanks — and doesn't care where they point their guns. He also likes food fights, and zero-gravity food fights are his favourite kind.

Dad: Strange things happen to me a lot, so I do have to have a few secrets from Dad. Sometimes, it's tricky to know which secrets you're keeping, and which ones you're sharing.

At the end of this story, I have a secret from Dad, but I'm not really sure whether I've kept my secret or whether he secretly knows my secret too. When you read it, you'll be able to decide what you think...

CHAPTER 2

We were making alien costumes at school. It was for our school play, and the play wasn't even supposed to be about aliens. It was supposed to be about animals, but Mrs Dribble, the art teacher, thinks we should all learn to express ourselves creatively.

That means coming up with our own ideas, and most of our ideas that day were about aliens.

I did think that sticking to the idea of animals might have been a better move, but once we started actually making the costumes, they looked really good.

There were big green aliens with lots of eyes, and little purple aliens with tentacles.

There were even some aliens that looked a little bit like animals, and Mrs. Dribble said they could go at the front so that people knew what the play was supposed to be about.

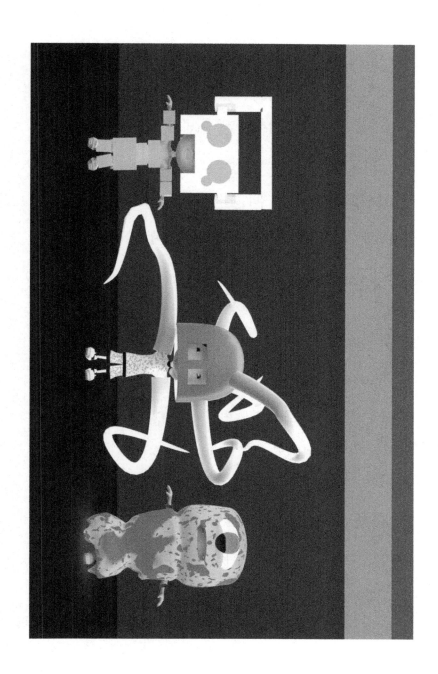

By the end of the day, our costumes were starting to look very good, and I was getting very keen on the idea of building things.

I think that was what made me have a really good look in the skip on the way home.

Skips are big yellow buckets which you sometimes find in roads. Grown-ups put all their most interesting rubbish in skips, and whenever I want to build anything really big I always look for parts in skips.

This skip was outside a house where there was a lot of building happening. The house was covered in scaffolding.

Scaffolding is like a climbing frame for builders, and it's supposed to keep them safe while they're building houses, but whenever Adam climbs on scaffolding, people shout at him that it isn't safe, so I don't really understand how that works.

Anyway, this skip was full of wood, and pipes, and rolls of shiny foil, and rolls of woolly stuff for keeping houses warm.

If the skip had come with instructions, I thought they would definitely be instructions for a tree house.

I told my brother, and he said, "Yes," and then he said, "...or a space station!"

we decided to build a tree house that looked exactly like a space station.

It took us quite a long time to carry all the bits from the skip to the big tree in the middle of the woods.

we decided to use the woods because we don't have a big tree in our garden, and because the tree house would stay very secret in the woods. This is because everyone thinks the woods are full of dinosaurs.

The woods aren't full of dinosaurs really. There are only a few dinosaurs, and they are only very small. (They are there because of an experiment I did a while ago, but that's in another story).

Anyway, we built the tree house using pieces of wood, but didn't look space station-y enough, so I used the woolly rolls on the inside to keep it warm. (Space is really cold) and I used the shiny foil on the outside because all space stations have a lot of shiny foil on them.

I made sure everything fitted together so that it didn't have any gaps (whenever there's a gap in a space station on a film, lots of alarms go off, and things get really bad). I used a roll of plastic to wrap the whole space station, and I even made a proper airlock door.

There was only one ladder in the skip. It only reached to the first few branches of the tree, so it wasn't high enough to get to the tree house.

The space station tree house looked great, but Adam kept asking when we were going to REALLY put it into space.

I thought about ladders all through tea time, but it was only when Dad read us Jack and the Beanstalk at bedtime that I had one of my brilliant ideas.

CHAPTER 3

I wrote an email to my friends:

Dear Friends,

I'm building a tree house space station.
You're all invited to it, but there is a problem.

Our ladder isn't long enough to get to the
tree house from the ground, so I need
more ladders.

Please leave any spare ladders in the skip next
to the wood, and tell anyone else you know
to do the same.

Love,
Jenny.

PS: don't worry if there are too many ladders -
I'll just think of something to do with any
extra ones.

we couldn't go to do more work on our treehouse until the weekend.

All week, people kept telling me they had found spare ladders and that they had passed the message on to other people...

I thought this was good, because it meant we would definitely have enough ladders.
But the Internet is a funny thing. I have found that when you put something onto the Internet, either nothing at all happens, or so much happens that you almost cannot believe it.

What happened this time was that everybody I knew passed the message onto everyone they knew. Then, everyone they knew passed it on to everyone THEY knew. And everyone who had a spare ladder brought it to the woods.

When we got there on Saturday morning, we found more ladders than I have ever seen in my whole life.

I haven't seen very many ladders before, actually — I've never been to the ladder version of Toys'R'Us, for example, but I think if I did go, it would look a bit like the skip next to the woods looked.

There were long metal ladders, and short, wooden ones. There were step ladders, and rope ladders, and extending ladders, and ladders that stretched, and ladders that folded. There were even some ladders on wheels, which looked like they would be either a lot of fun, or very dangerous.

There were just so many ladders that if we had a hundred space station tree houses, we could reach them all. In fact, even if the tree had been really, really tall, and the tree house had been really, really high up in it, we would still have been able to reach it with all our ladders.

I got Adam to help me carry all the ladders to the big tree. It took a very long time, and each time we came back, we saw more people arriving with more ladders they didn't want.

That was when I had another idea, and this one was a big one... Can you guess what it was?

CHAPTER 4

I got the idea from NASA, and from my brother. NASA Makes space rockets and space stations. A lot of really clever people are interested in space, so NASA has a lot of clever ideas.

The problem is that getting things into space is really hard. Not because space is a long way away - It's actually closer than Granny's house. Dad says it would only take half an hour to drive to space. The problem is that space is straight up, and you can't drive straight up.

That's why they use great big rockets.

Adam doesn't understand that getting to space is tricky, because he's too little, so he kept on and on asking me when we were going to put our space station into space.
Can you guess what my idea was yet?

We got the first ladder, and leant it against the trunk of the tree. Then we got the next ladder and carried it up. We tied it very tightly to the top of the first ladder so that it went all the way to where the treehouse was.

But we didn't stop there. We carried up the next ladder, and tied that to the top of the second ladder. By this time, the ladder reached so far up the tree, it stuck out the top of the highest branches.

Then we carefully carried the next ladder up and tied that on... And the next... and the next... and the next...

We just kept on going until the string of ladders reached right up into the sky. By now, it was quite wobbly at the top, and, when I looked down, I could see the whole town.

While I was looking, it got a bit windy, and the top of the ladder swooped backwards and forwards. I wobbled a bit, and had to grab on really tightly with both arms to stop myself from falling off.

I decided we probably needed to add some health and safety to our project, so we found some big hooks from the skip and used them to hook ourselves onto the ladders as we climbed up so that we couldn't fall off.

By teatime, we had both started to get very tired. The ladders had gone up right into the clouds, and climbing up and down was very difficult.

It was also very cold, and the inside of clouds is very wet (because they are made of rain).

Right at the top of our ladder, we got out of breath very quickly, and I started to get dizzy, so I decided we should stop for the day.

I remembered that the closer you get to space, the less air there is to breathe. I also decided I should do a little bit of Internet reading to see if there were any extra health and safety tips to think about before we got into space.

It turned out that there were quite a lot...

CHAPTER 5

I spent all evening reading about how difficult space was to explore, and thinking up ways to get around all the problems. It turned out to be very hard, but luckily we had found lots of helpful things in the skip, and I had made a list of them before we went home.

Problems with going to space:

- Space is very high up.
- The closer you get to space, the less air there is to breathe.
- The closer you get to space, the colder it gets.
- There is no gravity in space.

- Astronauts always throw their poo out of their spaceships, so there is a lot of poo floating around.
- There are no snacks in space. We must bring snacks.
- There may be aliens in space, but the Internet is not really sure.

Things we found in the skip:
- Lots of rubber pipes and hoses.
- A pair of dirty underpants.
- Rolls of silver insulation.
- Rolls of wool.
- Wood.
- Plastic.
- Some swimming masks and snorkels.
- Lots of rope.

- An old mattress.

- A broken bike.

- Some pieces of jigsaw.

- A sign saying, "Hats must be worn at all times."

I find that lists like this are a good way for me to come up with ideas.

At bedtime, Dad saw my lists on my bedside table.

He said, "What are you two up to, then? Is it something I should know about?"

I just Acted Normal, and said, "We're just playing." Then I said, "by the way, can you print out a sewing pattern for me?"

Dad said, "OK..."

I said, "One for a onesie in my size, and in Adam's size. It has to have arms and a hood, and socks."

Dad nodded, but he looked a little bit puzzled, and said, "I hope you're playing safely."

I said, "Yes, I'm thinking a lot about being safe," and it was true. It was all about being safe.

On Sunday, I knew we had a lot of work to do so we ran down to the woods quite early.

The first thing we needed was a way to stay warm because space is cold even when it's a really nice day.

I had brought some scissors from home, and I used the patterns Dad had printed out for me to cut out, and make, onesie space suits.

I used some of the silver insulation material for the outside (because it looked really spacey) and the woolly material on the inside. Then, I sewed the masks and snorkels, from the skip, into the hoods.

Then, I connected the ends of the snorkels to a long, long piece of the rubber pipe, and taped the other end to the bottom of the ladder.

Our space suits made it a bit more difficult to climb the ladder, but they were very warm. Also, because the rubber pipe went to the bottom of the ladder, we didn't get out of breath even when we climbed up to the top of the ladder.

By lunchtime, we had put up enough ladders to get above the cloud.

We sat on the top, and had our picnic. We could see clouds underneath us like a big, fluffy carpet, going all the way into the distance, and above us, the sky was dark and full of stars. (It was only lunch time, but it's always dark in space).

After lunch, things started getting easier.

There were two reasons for this:

1) The higher we got, the less gravity there was, so it was easier to climb.

and

2) I had the idea to use some bits of broken bike to make a sort of pulley - so that all Adam had to do was sit at the

bottom, and tie new ladders onto a rope. Then, he could pull the other end of the rope, and the ladders would get dragged up to the top, for me to attach.

Eventually, everything got so light that I could float next to the ladders while I tied them on and, when I looked down, I could see the whole, round shape of the Earth underneath me.

I was really in space!

The next job was to bring up our space station tree house.
I had to make a better pulley to do that, because the treehouse was very big and heavy, so I used all the gears from the

broken bike, and put them together, so that I could use the pedals to wind the rope round, and haul the space station up the ladder.

It was very tiring, and I had to keep stopping.

By the time I saw it coming up through the clouds, towards me, my legs were completely worn out.

I only just had enough energy to tie it to the top of the ladder, and put a rubber pipe into it. (We had to get air into our space station all the way from the ground with a big rubber pipe, like our snorkels).

Then, I left the space station, and climbed slowly all the way back down to the ground.

The next day at school, I invited everyone to a party in space....

CHAPTER 6

All my friends wanted to come, but a few of them have been told, by their parents, that they can't go on adventures with me (that is because strange things happen to me a lot, and some grown-ups don't like dinosaurs, or zombie robots, or locking the Prime Minister in a fairground ride).

They mostly came anyway, but just Acted Normal, when their parents asked where they were going.

It took me quite a long time to make space suits for everyone, but they were all very pleased with them when they were finished, and we all started climbing up to the space station.

The climb went quite well, and only three people decided they were a bit scared of heights, and had to climb back down again before they got to the clouds.

A couple more got a bit scared when it started getting windy, and the ladder wobbled and wobbled, but by that time, everyone was tied onto the ladder, so getting down would have been even harder than carrying on.

Eventually, we all got to the space station, and we climbed in through the airlock, and took off our space suits.

Inside, it was a bit cold, but there was plenty of air and no gravity, so we had a great time.

If you have never been to a party in space, next time you are invited to one, you really should go.

We started by having a flying, swimming race from one side of the space station to the other. In zero-gravity, you can swim through the air.

My friend Alfred raced Adam. Alfred is bigger than Adam, and he used his feet to spring away from the wall and float across with his arm out, pretending to be Superman. Adam used his arms like a helicopter, so he started slowly, but he just kept getting faster, and faster, until he crashed into the other wall.

Then we played flying tag, and alien bulldog, and, "What's the time, Mr. Asteroid?"
Then, Alison looked out of the window, and said, "Look! A spaceship."

We all crowded round (which is hard to do in zero gravity, because you keep bouncing off everything). It wasn't a spaceship. It was another space station, floating by in the distance.

The other space station was a grown-up one, which I'd seen on the TV lots of times. It was called the International Space Station, and it had astronauts living in it, all the time. They do science experiments, which sound like fun, but I'd also seen them eating, which also looked like fun.

That reminded me that we'd bought some snacks.

The first thing Adam did was to open a can of fizzy drink. That was a very bad idea.

On the way up the ladder, the can must have got swished about in the wind and juddered around, while we were climbing. It also must have got spun around a lot, when we were floating around the space station.

When Adam opened the can, the drink went everywhere.

When people say something "went everywhere" they don't usually mean it, because we have gravity most of the time, and, "everywhere" usually means "on the floor."

When something goes everywhere in space, it really does go everywhere!

The foamy spray squirted out of the can, and hit EVERY SINGLE WALL. Then, it bounced off the walls and hit EVERY SINGLE PERSON in the space station. Imagine something splashing, but then not stopping until it splashed off something else. That was what it was like.

The foamy bits of orange drink kept splashing, and splashing, and splashing, for ages, but even once they'd finished splashing, they drifted and span through the air, like long wet bubbly strings, and wobbly orange balls of drink, which bubbled and fizzed.

Adam and Alfred thought this was great, and Adam opened another can of green drink right away (but not before he'd given it a good shake). Everyone started swimming around the space station, trying to gulp down drops of drink.

Then someone opened a bag of crisps, and someone else opened a packet of M&Ms, and they all rattled into the air, like little asteroids, and we all started trying to catch them in our mouths.

That was when Alfred and Adam found the rest of the snacks, and decided to start a food fight.

I'm not going to even try to describe what a food fight is like in zero gravity, but I think if you stop reading for a minute and imagine it, you'll probably get the idea.

When you've finished thinking about that, we'll start a new chapter about what happened next time I went to the space station.

Start reading again soon, though, because that was when I met the alien...

CHAPTER 7

At first, we didn't realise that it was an alien at all. We thought that the food fight had been a little bit messier than we realised.

It looked like there was a huge tangle of spaghetti floating around the space station.

Then, I remembered that we hadn't taken any spaghetti for snacks (spaghetti is a messy snack even when there is gravity).
Also, I noticed that the giant spaghetti monster had eyes, so I realised he must be an alien.

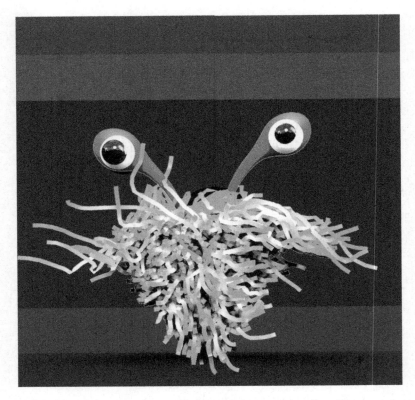

That was when I got a bit scared. The only aliens I had ever seen before were on TV and they were ALWAYS trying to take over the Earth, or chase people. The one thing I knew from TV about aliens was that they were ALWAYS baddies.

I always have my cleverest ideas when things get really bad, and I decided that the best thing would be to keep our space-suits on, and open the door so that all the air (and the giant spaghetti monster) got sucked out into space.

I grabbed the door handle, and started to try to tell my brother what my plan was.

But my brother wasn't listening. Instead, he was taking his mask off.

"Hello!" he said to the alien, "I'm Adam."

That's when I found out that not all aliens are baddies.

The alien said, "Hello," back. It didn't actually say it with its mouth (because it didn't have a mouth). Instead, it spelled it out by making letter shapes with its spaghetti arms. If you have ever had a conversation with a plate of alphabetti spaghetti, it was a bit like that.

The alien explained that it had seen the Earth from its home (it lived in a place called Sutton, which is on Saturn) and it wanted to visit Earth. It had first gone to the grown-up space station, but when it had looked through the windows, it had seen all the flashing lights, and the serious people doing experiments, and it had got a bit frightened.

It had thought that our space station looked a bit friendlier.

That was when I felt sorry for thinking about sucking the alien out into space. I try to do GOOD things if I can and that definitely would not have been a good thing. If I had done that, I would have been the baddie!

"We have to go to school," I told the alien, "but we can come and see you later."

"Would you like to see our school?" said Adam.

The Alien spelt out, "Yes!" (It even did the exclamation mark, so it must have really wanted to come.

I wasn't too sure that was a good idea, but the alien had made up its mind, so we all climbed down the ladder together, and went to school.

Nobody really saw us on the way to school (although a few people who did ran away very quickly). When we got there, we introduced the alien to Alfred, and it was very quickly surrounded by lots of our friends.

That was probably why none of the grown-ups saw the alien, until assembly....

The whole school was in assembly and we were all listening to a talk about, "Thinking of others."

The main point of the talk seemed to be that thinking of others was good, and being selfish was bad, but we already knew all about that, because grown-ups talk about that A LOT. I think they need to remind themselves about it, ALL THE TIME, in case they forget, and start being selfish.

Anyway, we had told the alien to stay outside during assembly, but it must have got a bit bored, because it came in, right in the middle, and squelched down on the floor, in between Adam and Alfred.

I hoped nobody would notice, but it was a giant spaghetti monster, so as it turned out, EVERYBODY noticed.

I put my hand up to explain, but I didn't get the chance because, soon, all the teachers, and all the children who hadn't already met the alien, started running around shouting and screaming.

This was not good...

CHAPTER 8

Pretty soon, everyone in the whole school had run away.

The only people left were the few friends who had already met the alien in the playground - plus, of course, Adam and I, and the alien (who didn't really understand what all the fuss was about).

We were left all alone, in the school hall, and one of the teachers had locked the doors, on the way out.

They must have thought the alien was a baddie, but I think locking the doors was selfish, because if the alien really had been a baddie, then they would have locked us all in with it.

They must have done it because they were scared, but being scared is not a good reason to be selfish.

Anyway, we all watched out of the window, as all the teachers and the other children ran out of the school gates, and shut them.
Then, everybody stood outside, and watched to see what would happen.

One of the teachers was calling someone on her mobile phone, and I had a nasty feeling I knew who it was she was calling.

Shutting the school gates was another selfish thing to do, but it was also a bit pointless. Lots of strange things happen to me, and I already know that breaking through the school gates is easy.

In other stories, I have already seen my Dad's car, and some zombie robots, and a flood smash through them. A giant spaghetti monster would have no problem breaking through them if it wanted to.

But the spaghetti monster didn't want to break anything. It just sat in the corner, spelling out words like "sad" and "lonely" and "home."

I was trying to think of a way to get the alien home, when Adam suddenly looked out of the window, and said, "Oh, goody!"

When Adam says, "Oh, goody!" it doesn't often mean anything good.   It usually means something big and messy.

This time, it meant the army had arrived. It's sometimes good news when the army arrives, but this time, it wasn't. The teacher must have phoned the army and told them there was an alien in the school.
The army must have been as scared as everyone else, and decided to come with lots of tanks and guns.

They were all standing outside the school deciding which type of gun to use first. (I would have used the rocket launchers first, but, luckily, it wasn't up to me).

Then an army man's voice came through a very big loudspeaker, "THE ALIEN MUST COME OUT WITH ITS HANDS UP! YOU

HAVE TEN MINUTES OR WE WILL START SHOOTING!" It said.

I thought that sounded a bit rude, and anyway, the spaghetti monster didn't have any hands.

The spaghetti monster got up, slithered sadly over to the window, and got ready to climb out.

That was when I had one of my ideas. For some reason, when things are really bad, and when I'm really scared, I have my best ideas.

I said, "Can you lift us up to the ceiling?" The spaghetti monster made the word "Yes!" Then, it stretched itself out like a long rope, and helped me climb up to the ceiling of the hall. I pushed one of the ceiling tiles up, and crawled into the space above the ceiling.

"Come on," I said to everyone, "we have to go to the art room."

Everybody climbed up after me, and we all crawled along the dirty, spidery place above the ceiling until we got out of the hall, and into the ceiling of the art room. (I already knew how to get there, because we had done this before when I accidentally flooded the school during the Christmas play.)

Anyway, when we all climbed down into the art room, I explained my plan to everyone.
Can you guess what my idea was?

CHAPTER 9

Remember how we had been making costumes, in Mrs. Dribble's class, for our play about animals?

And remember how we had all had the idea to make alien costumes instead?

Well, I told everyone to get dressed up in the alien costumes. We didn't look exactly like aliens, because our costumes were a bit home-made, and some of them hadn't been finished. But that was good. I didn't want people to think we were REALLY aliens. That was sort of the point.

I sent Adam out first. He was dressed as a green, blobby alien with one big eye.

We all watched, from the window, as he walked out into the middle of the playground.

All the army guns pointed at him, and everybody held their breath. I started to think he might look too much like an alien after all.

Then, he took off his alien head, and started to laugh.

Then, all the kids watching started to laugh. Then, the teachers. Then, the army started to laugh.

Then, Alfred went out in his purple alien suit with lots of tentacles. The army all pointed their guns again, and then started laughing again when one of his tentacles fell off, because it was only made of bits of rubbish, stuck together.

One by one, we all went out and stood in the playground in our alien costumes, and everybody laughed, and cheered. We even did a little alien dance, pretending to be scary, and at the end, everyone clapped.

By the time the real alien came out of the school, the army were packing up and driving away. Nobody noticed that one of the aliens was a bit more realistic than all the others, and was actually a giant spaghetti monster.

By now, all the parents had come to collect their children, and everyone was showing off their alien costumes to their mums and dads, so they didn't take any notice of Adam and I leading the giant spaghetti monster away.

I thought we had escaped, but then I saw Dad. He had come to pick us up!
"Hello," said Dad, "and who's this under here?"
Dad started looking a bit too closely at the spaghetti monster. He touched one of its spaghetti tentacles. It must have felt a bit

more real than he expected, because he looked a bit confused.

I just Acted Normal, and said, "Can we walk our friend home?"

I was really pleased with that question, because it meant I didn't actually have to tell Dad about the alien, and I didn't have to lie either. I didn't have to say, "Our friend is an alien," or say, "our friend is not an alien," I just had to ask if we could walk our friend home. Dad still looked a bit confused, "Where is your friend from?" he asked.

"Sutton!" I said, and smiled my best Act Normal smile.

Adam said "Sutton is on Saturn!" I made my smile even bigger, as if Adam was being silly.

Dad looked right at me, then he looked at all the crowds around the school. Then, he looked at the army people all getting into their tanks around us. Then, he looked at the spaghetti monster.

I wasn't quite sure what Dad was thinking about, but he had a serious face.

Then, he smiled an Act Normal smile right back at me, and said, "I think you'd better get your friend home as quickly as you can." So, while Dad chatted to the other parents about how good our costumes were, Adam and I took the spaghetti monster back to the woods, and up into the tree, and up the ladder into space....

CHAPTER 10

Adam and I hid the bottom ladder, but we didn't take down the rest. We said goodbye to the spaghetti monster, and we all decided that grown-ups were probably not ready to meet aliens yet.

But, we left the rest of the ladders there, because it's handy to have a space station, and I've got lots of space adventures planned for the future.

I've been thinking a lot about how scared everyone was of the alien, and how I was scared when I first met it, and how I had the idea of letting all the air out of the space station, because I thought the alien was a baddie. I've been wondering why I have my cleverest ideas when I'm scared.

I've also been thinking a lot about "Jack and the Beanstalk."

I still don't like Jack very much, but I think I understand the moral of the story a bit better now.

It's not that stealing and killing are right, or that it's OK to behave stupidly.

It's that when you're scared, it gets easier to be clever, but it gets harder to be good.

The end.

Act Normal and read more...

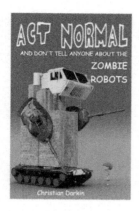

Made in the USA
Columbia, SC
20 August 2023

21884567R00050